THE FOX WHO FOOLED THE MONK

33 Zen Stories to Stop Overthinking, Release Negative Thoughts, and Find Peace & Happiness in Letting Go

Zen Tales

Book 2

KAI TSUKIMI

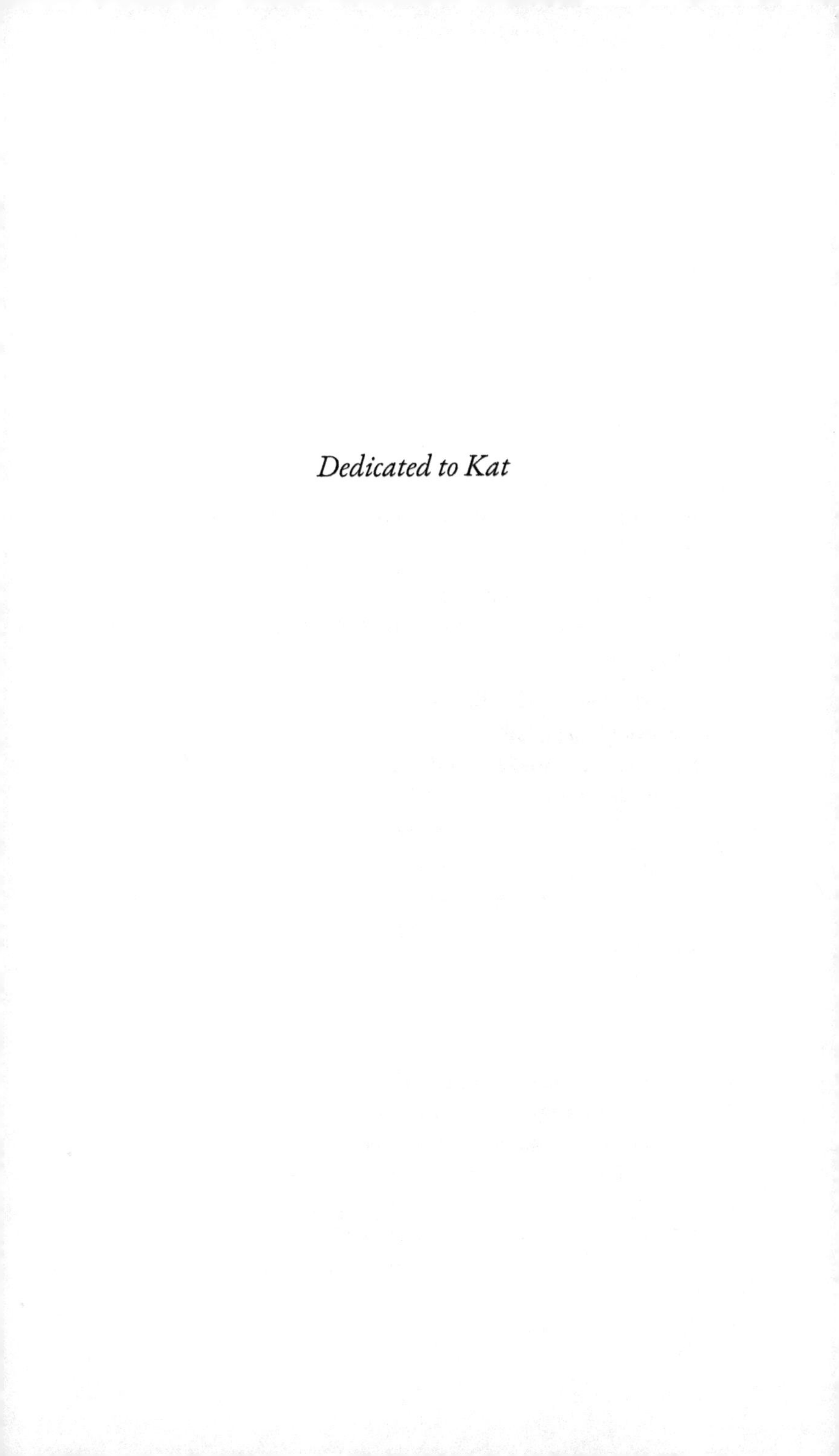

Dedicated to Kat

A book can shift your perspective, but a ritual can transform your life. As a thank-you for reading, I'd like to offer you our exclusive *Zen Clarity Kit*, designed to help you clear your mind, refocus, and make Zen teachings a part of your daily routine.

What's Inside the Kit?

✓ **The Zen Morning Ritual Guide** – A simple daily practice to anchor your mind in stillness.

✓ **A 5-Minute Audio Meditation** – Gently guide yourself into a state of clarity and focus.

✓ **Zen Minimalism Wallpapers** – Subtle reminders to cultivate presence throughout your day.

>> Scan the QR Code or click here
to download your free gift <<

Table of Contents

Introduction

What Is Zen?

If you ask ten Zen masters what Zen is, you'll get ten different answers—and none of them will satisfy you.

One might say it's the sound of bamboo in the wind.

Another might hit you with a stick.

Another might ask you where your thoughts go when you stop thinking.

The more you search for a definition, the more it slips through your fingers. Zen isn't a belief. It's not a technique. It isn't even something you "get."

It's what's already here—before the question.

It's the silence between thoughts, the feeling before the answer, the pause between one breath and the next.

And in this book, it takes the shape of a fox.

Why a Fox?

Because if Zen ever decided to play tricks, it would likely wear a red tail.

The fox is clever. Mysterious. It shows up when you're not looking, then vanishes when you reach for it. It leaves footprints on the ceiling, eats your lunch without asking, and stares at you like it knows something you don't.

In Japanese and Chinese folklore, foxes are shape-shifters—beings of mischief and magic. In Zen, too, the fox is no stranger. There are old koans where a monk becomes a fox for five hundred lifetimes, and others where a fox speaks human words. Not as metaphors. As facts.

The fox in this book might be your teacher. Or it might be your own mind playing tricks. It might show you how to stop overthinking, or it might lead you in circles until you give up entirely. And that surrender... might be the beginning of peace.

What Are Zen Stories?

Zen stories don't behave.

They aren't here to inspire you, comfort you, or fix you. In fact, they're not "here" at all—not in the usual way.

They're sudden, strange, sometimes funny, sometimes sharp. Like the fox, they appear in the middle of your assumptions and start digging holes.

They don't offer answers. They offer openings.

This book is a collection of 33 Zen stories, following a solitary monk who retreats into the forest in search of clarity, stillness, and simplicity—only to find a wild fox already waiting for him.

The stories are short. Often surreal. Some are haunting. Others are absurd. Many are both.

But together, they form a quiet mirror—a way to see your thoughts, your habits, your distractions, and your presence reflected in unexpected ways. You may feel confused. Or strangely understood. Or like you've been tricked into waking up.

That's the fox's way.

How to Use This Book

There is no map. No order. No beginning or end.

You can read the stories in sequence, or skip around like a fox darting through trees. You can linger on one for days, or forget it as soon as it's finished. Both are fine.

At the end of each part, you'll find a few gentle questions —not to analyze the stories, but to open them further. You may feel something. You may feel nothing. But if you notice yourself trying to figure them out, pause. Smile. The fox got you again.

The purpose of this book is not to solve Zen.

It's to loosen the knots that keep you tangled in your own mind.

To show you that peace doesn't come from control, or answers, or constant thought.

It comes from stopping long enough to see what's already true.

So sit down. Let your shoulders drop.

Breathe in, breathe out.

And let the fox show you the path by walking off it.

Because the clarity you're searching for isn't hiding.

You're just too busy looking.

— *Kai*

PART I

Where Paw Meets Porch

For things to reveal themselves to us, we need to be ready to abandon our views about them.

Thich Nhat Hanh

1

———

THE CABIN WITH NO LOCK

THE MONK ARRIVED AT DUSK.

He stood at the edge of the clearing, breath curling into the cool air, robes brushing the wild grasses at his feet. Before him stood a crooked wooden cabin, small and slouched, as if leaning in to hear something the trees refused to reveal.

It was humbler than he'd imagined.

The roof sagged under a patchwork of moss. The window shutters hung crooked on tired hinges. And the door, strangely, hung ajar—open just wide enough to suggest it had never fully closed.

He had come seeking silence, fleeing the endless debates of the temple that had left his heart worn thin. He thought the forest would be empty. But as he took a step toward the cabin, a faint rustle stirred the grasses behind him—too brief to be wind, too deliberate to be chance.

He paused, listening. The sound did not return.

Drawing closer, he reached for where a latch or lock should have been. His hand hovered at the edge of the weathered frame. There was nothing—no hook, no bar, no barrier between him and whatever might already live inside.

He lingered, the elder's words rising like breath:

"The woods are not empty just because they are quiet."

He glanced once toward the darkening trees, half-expecting to catch a glint of eyes watching from the undergrowth. But there was only the deepening blue of twilight.

With a steadying breath, he pressed his palm to the door.

It gave way easily.

Inside: a thin mat, a low table, and the faint damp of cedar.

The room felt untouched, yet not entirely abandoned.

And on the table, small enough to miss if he hadn't already been looking for something—anything—a single red whisker lay in the last light of day.

The monk sat slowly on the mat, crossing his legs, resting his hands in his lap. He closed his eyes, steadying his breath as he had done countless times before. And yet, something in him leaned toward the door—just slightly —as if part of him already knew he was not the first visitor that day.

$$2$$

THE BOWL OF SILENCE

THE MONK ROSE BEFORE THE FIRST LIGHT. HE folded his blanket without sound, lit no candle, and slid open the cabin door to let the cold morning breathe into the room.

As the trees shifted from shadow to shape, he carried an old wooden bowl outside and placed it on the porch. He did not fill it with rice or tea. He simply set it there, empty. A small ritual he had carried from the temple, though no teacher had ever given it to him.

At the monastery, it had been different. Bowls were filled and refilled—grains, vegetables, bitter tea. But those offerings had always come with murmurs, with the scrape of sandals on stone, with the weight of eyes watching to see if you bowed correctly.

Here, the empty bowl felt cleaner somehow. A gesture not toward gods or ancestors, but toward space itself.

The monk sat facing it, his breath slow and even, letting the sound of the forest settle into his bones. A crow called from somewhere unseen. A branch creaked under the weight of unseen wind.

And then—

a feather.

Black as riverstone, damp with dew, it drifted from above and landed soundlessly in the bowl's hollow center. The monk's breath caught in his throat. He watched it settle, its tip quivering as if it still carried the motion of unseen wings.

He did not move to touch it.

The forest held its breath.

Or perhaps, it had never been breathing at all.

When the sun touched the tops of the trees, the monk stood and left the feather where it lay.

Later, when he returned to bring the bowl inside, it was empty again.

No feather.

No trace.

Just the bowl, waiting as though it had never held anything at all.

From the shadowed trees, a fox flicked its tail, eyes glinting at the monk who sat with an empty bowl and saw only a feather's dance.

3

―――

THE APPLE LEFT UNFINISHED

IT BEGAN WITH AN APPLE.

Not a full one, not a perfect offering—but half-eaten, left neatly on the monk's meditation cushion just after dawn. The bite was clean, curved with small teeth, and the flesh still white. Whoever had left it hadn't been gone long.

He stood in the doorway, staring at it for a full minute.

Then, without a word, he picked it up, stepped outside, and threw it into the trees.

It thudded against a trunk and vanished into the undergrowth.

He did not meditate that morning.

The next day, he rose earlier, lit no lantern, and opened the cabin door with a slow, deliberate calm. The cushion was empty. He allowed himself a small breath of satisfaction.

But when he returned from fetching water, there it was again.

Another apple. Another bite. Same teeth. Same stillness.

This time, he carried it outside in both hands and placed it on a rock at the edge of the clearing, as if offering it back to whoever—or whatever—had delivered it.

On the third day, there were two apples.

Both bitten. One placed where he usually sat.

The other, balanced perfectly atop the old bell on the altar.

He sat on the floor instead.

He did not ring the bell.

By the fourth day, the apples weren't just bitten—they were arranged.

One lay at the center of the cushion.

One balanced on the windowsill.

A third perched on the stack of firewood, tilted at an impossible angle, as if daring gravity to intervene.

The monk stood in the doorway with his arms folded and whispered, "Why?"

Not to the forest.

Not to the apples.

But to the part of himself that still believed this could be solved.

That night, he lit no fire. He waited in the dark, sitting upright with the cushion beside him—empty, finally. He kept his eyes open as long as he could, trying to catch the moment of arrival.

He fell asleep without knowing it.

When he woke at dawn, the cushion was once again occupied.

Not with an apple.

With a small pile of seeds.

Dozens of them. Arranged in a spiral.

He sat down on the floorboards, legs crossed, back straight.

This time, he didn't move them.

He didn't ask.

Outside the window, just for a moment, a pair of red ears dipped below the tall grass.

4

———

THE BARK THAT WOULDN'T BURN

THE MONK WOKE TO THE BITE OF COLD AIR pressing through the cabin walls. It was the kind of morning that hummed beneath the skin—sharp, thin as frost on bare wood.

He wrapped his robe tightly and stepped outside. Breath moved visibly before him in soft, steady clouds, each one rising and vanishing into the trees. He walked to the far side of the clearing, feet sinking into damp earth scattered with pine needles and broken twigs.

Near a collapsed tree, half-buried under fallen branches, he gathered wood. The logs were wet but solid, thick with sap that clung to his fingers.

That's when he noticed it.

A branch that didn't quite belong.

Lighter than the others, smoother, almost polished. It lay

near a faint indent in the dew—like a paw's brief mark, already softening in the morning light.

He turned it over in his hands. It smelled faintly of something he could not name. Almost like dry fur warmed by sun. He shook the thought loose before it could root itself.

Back inside, he stacked the wood beside the hearth—edges aligned, weight balanced—just as he had in the temple, where masters scolded uneven piles as flaws in the soul. He placed the pale branch last, laying it on top as though saving it for something he couldn't name.

The fire built itself slowly. Thick, damp branches first. Then thinner, drier ones that cracked and hissed as they caught. Warmth stretched through the room, loosening his chest, easing the night's ache.

When the coals glowed steady and hot, he reached for the pale branch. He held it a moment longer than necessary, then placed it in the heart of the flame.

It did not catch.

He turned it. Shifted it. Broke it in half and laid the pieces side by side. The fire curled around it but found no hold.

Smoke thickened. The other logs burned clean, embers rising like small stars in the dim light. But the pale branch remained cold, untouched, as if it belonged to no element at all.

He tried again.

And again.

And again.

At last, he let the fire die, embers settle, effort unravel.

He left the pale branch resting on the ash, half-surrendered to nothing.

That night, he dreamed.

Soft footsteps circling the cabin.

Something brushing against the doorframe.

And laughter—not cruel, but not kind—curling through the cracks like smoke, trailing a glimpse of a red tail in the moonlight.

By morning, the hearth was cold.

The fire had long surrendered to the night.

He knelt, expecting to find the pale branch still where he had left it.

But it was gone.

In its place, nestled against the ash, lay a single tuft of red fur—soft, curled, impossibly bright in the grey light of dawn.

He did not touch it.

Not yet.

Beyond the cabin, a fox crouched in the frost, its breath a faint cloud, amused by the monk who had spent the night tending a fire that could not touch its gift.

5

———

THE PAWPRINT THAT WAS NOT THERE

THE MONK DIDN'T TOUCH THE TUFT OF RED FUR by the hearth. Not at first.

He let it sit there all morning while he swept the floor, boiled water, and restacked the firewood—tasks done with the temple's precision, where certainty was a virtue the masters praised. But no matter how many times he passed by, his eyes kept returning to that single curl of fur —too bright, too deliberate, too placed.

By midday, he lifted it with the edge of his sleeve, holding it between two fingers as though it might dissolve if he breathed too hard.

He placed it on the shelf above the small altar, next to the old bell that hadn't rung in years. A small offering to whatever game was being played.

That night, after the lantern refused him again, he let the fire burn low. He sat in the dark, listening to the small sounds of the forest, the faint creak of the cabin's bones, the weight of his own breath in the room.

At some hour he could not name, he rose and stirred the cooling ash with the tip of a stick, as if searching for something he had missed.

That's when he saw it—

a single pawprint, pressed perfectly in the grey dust.

Small. Delicate. Fox.

He stared, time blurring.

Proof.

Finally, something real. Something he could point to, touch, name.

But when he woke the next morning and reached to show himself—

the ash was smooth again, undisturbed, as though no print had ever been there at all.

He stirred the ash once more, slower this time, more careful.

Nothing.

He knelt back, heart sinking beyond confusion.

The next night, after the fire burned down once again, he leaned close to the hearth.

A faint rustle stirred outside, and there it was—the same pawprint, pressed in the ash.

He leaned even closer, almost smiling.

Caught you, he thought.

But when he blinked—just once—

the print was gone.

No trace.

No mark.

No proof.

He laughed, but there was no humor in it.

Just breath and bone and the quiet unraveling of what he thought he knew.

He sat back against the wall, staring into the dark hearth, half-expecting the pawprint to return the moment he closed his eyes.

He almost hoped it wouldn't, his breath steadying as he let the need for proof slip.

In the forest's hush, a crow tilted its head, watching the fox nose the cabin's edge, scattering ash with a single breath before slipping into the night, amused by the monk who chased its fleeting mark.

6

THE LANTERN THAT WOULDN'T STAY LIT

THE MONK WAITED FOR DUSK TO SETTLE, sitting cross-legged on the floor as long shadows stretched across the cabin walls. The forest had been unusually still all afternoon, as if something unseen was holding its breath.

When darkness finally folded itself over the clearing, he stood and reached for the small oil lantern hanging by the door. His fingers moved carefully, as they always had—steady, practiced, unshaken by the day's silence. A steadiness honed in the temple, where lanterns burned without fail under watchful masters.

He lit the wick with ease, shielding the flame with his palm as it grew steady and bright.

For a moment, the light held.

As he set the lantern on the window ledge, the flame flickered once, then vanished, snuffed by nothing he could name.

He relit it, slower this time, as if gentleness might persuade it to stay.

Again, the flame rose—soft and golden against the dark.

Again, it died.

He checked the wick.

Checked the oil.

Checked the glass for cracks.

Everything as it should be.

No wind. No draft.

Nothing but stillness.

He tried again.

And again.

Each time, the flame returned—brief, hopeful—only to vanish the moment he let go.

His jaw tightened, breath short. His hands, once steady, began to tremble—not with fear, but with something sharper, smaller. A coil of frustration tightening around his ribs.

He lit the lantern one final time, holding it longer than before, daring it to flicker, daring it to stay.

And then—

from just beyond the window,

a soft, breathy sound.

Not wind.

Not branch.

Not bird.

Something closer.

He stepped toward the window, pressing his face to the glass, peering into the night.

For a breath, he saw nothing.

And then—just at the edge of the clearing—a red tail, low and swaying, slipping into the dark.

The lantern's flame wavered, danced once more, and without warning, snuffed itself out.

The monk stood in the dark, gripping the cold frame of the window, his heart quickening, the tension pulling tighter.

Beyond the clearing, the fox paused, its red tail flicking, eyes glinting with quiet delight at the monk whose light it had stolen.

7

———

WHERE STILLNESS WAS STARED DOWN

THE MONK OPENED THE DOOR BEFORE SUNRISE, expecting the hush of the clearing, the soft rustle of leaves, maybe the ghost of a breeze passing through the trees.

Instead, the fox was sitting on the porch.

Its body was small, more shadow than shape in the grey light, but its eyes—those were not morning eyes. They were deep, alert, glinting with a kind of stillness that didn't belong to the forest.

For a moment, the monk felt nothing.

No fear. No surprise.

Only the simple registering of what stood before him.

He straightened his spine, folded his hands.

He had sat with thunder.

He had breathed through pain.

He had endured silence for weeks without breaking, lessons carved in the temple, where masters taught the mind to hold steady.

A fox, even a bold one, could not disturb him.

But the fox didn't move.

It simply watched him, as if it had been waiting for this exact hour, this exact light, this exact monk in this exact doorway. Its ears flicked once. Its tail curled neatly beside its paws.

The monk held the gaze.

Then a flicker.

Not in the fox—in him.

Something unsettled began to rise. Not fear. Not quite.

A tightening in the chest, like the breath was still flowing but not fully reaching the lungs.

The fox's gaze didn't waver. If anything, it deepened—playful, bright, and utterly unreadable.

The monk exhaled longer than necessary.

He found himself shifting slightly in place, his fingers no longer folded but curling around each other. The silence no longer felt serene. It was taut, coiled like string around something invisible.

The fox tilted its head.

The monk took a step forward.

And in a blink—the fox was gone, a faint rustle fading into the trees.

No scurry.

The monk stood alone in the soft blue hush of dawn, heart louder than it should've been.

He turned back into the cabin.

And there, arranged in a perfect line across the floor:

A single black feather.

A patch of red fur.

A half-eaten apple.

And just beside them, pressed into the smooth dust of the floorboards—a pawprint.

A signature.

Nothing more.

Nothing less.

From the forest's edge, a villager paused, gathering wood, her eyes catching the cabin's open door, where traces lay like an offering, left by a fox she'd never see.

8

———

THE CUSHION SHARED

THE MORNING AIR WAS THICK WITH THE SMELL of pine and old rain. He had wandered long, tracing a narrow trail that curved between moss-covered stones and long-forgotten trees. He returned just after the mist had begun to lift, dew still clinging to the cuffs of his robe.

The cabin door was slightly ajar.

Not wide. Just enough.

A faint trail of dew-damp pawprints gleamed on the porch.

As if something had entered—quietly, confidently—and not bothered to close it behind.

He stepped inside without sound.

And stopped.

The fox was there.

Perched on the meditation cushion, one paw lightly tapping its edge, as if testing its claim. Eyes half-open, glinting with a quiet dare. Breathing slow, yet poised.

The monk froze, still as stone.

His heart stuttered, a temple-taught rhythm faltering, as if the cushion's theft knocked something loose inside him.

The cushion had been his only claim of structure, an anchor, where silence was shaped by ritual.

Where he placed his body, met the silence, and resisted distraction.

Now the fox sat in the center of it, as if it had been his all along.

The monk stayed at the threshold, watching.

The fox didn't flinch. Didn't glance up. It simply continued—breathing in, breathing out—tail tucked close, ears flicking occasionally in response to sounds the monk couldn't hear.

Something in him wanted to shoo it away.

Something older in him knew better.

So he crossed the room and sat beside the cushion—on the floor, without ceremony, spine soft. His knees creaked. His body folded into itself. He closed his eyes.

The silence shifted.

For a long time, they breathed together.

Each breath distinct, yet tangled, like two currents carving one stream.

A single apple seed, unnoticed, rolled from the fox's fur, clicking faintly against the floor—a sound neither near nor far, breaking nothing, holding everything.

The fox yawned once, low and slow, then rose.

It stepped off the cushion without a glance, without sound, and walked past the monk, its body brushing lightly against his shoulder.

The cabin door creaked.

By the time he opened his eyes, the fox was gone.

He looked down at the cushion.

A single red hair lay coiled at its center, catching the light.

He sat in its place, not to reclaim it, but to continue something unnamed.

And for the first time in weeks, he felt no need to light the lantern, check the hearth, or sweep the floor.

He just sat.

Reflection Questions

What does it feel like to sit with something you can't explain or control?

Have you ever mistaken stillness for solitude?

What traces has life left on your path lately—feathers, fur, fruit, or footprints?

How do you react when your ritual is interrupted?

Use every distraction as an object of meditation and they cease to be distractions.

Mingyur Rinpoche

9

———

THE ROOF THAT TILTED TOWARD THE MOON

IT BEGAN WITH A CREAK.

A long, low groan from somewhere above the monk's head—deep in the rafters or behind the beams, like the cabin itself was shifting in its sleep. He paused mid-step, teacup in hand, and looked up. The ceiling stared back with blank timber and quiet cobwebs.

That night, as he sat in meditation, the moonlight poured in through the east window as it always had. But instead of falling in its usual pool at the center of the floor, it spilled upward—slanting along the far wall at an impossible angle, illuminating a stack of firewood that had never held the moon before.

He adjusted the cushion. Shifted his seat.

Still off.

He stood.

Tilted his head.

Maybe it was the moon. Lower tonight. Or higher.

But when he fetched the old lever from the storeroom and placed it along the window sill, the bubble hung crooked—off by enough to see, and just enough to deny.

The next morning brought another creak, sharper this time. He swept the floor carefully, eyes scanning the grain of the boards. One plank, perfectly flush just days ago, now curled slightly upward at one end, humped like something beneath it had started to breathe.

That night, the moonlight didn't touch the floor at all.

It climbed the wall and spilled onto the beams.

Bent.

Ascending.

The monk climbed to the roof the following day, jaw tight, hands full of tools. The sky stretched taut above him—too wide, too empty, as if pulling at the angles of the world itself.

From the ridge, he could see the cabin's spine had shifted. A dip, then a rise, the whole structure leaning subtly toward the trees. Or toward the moon.

He hammered. Measured. Nudged things back into place.

His hands shook. Tools slipped.

The hammer struck wrong, again and again, as if mocking his effort—his need to force order onto a world that refused to hold still.

That evening, the moonlight poured upward. The room felt off-center, slanted in its bones.

At dusk, he climbed the roof again—no longer to fix, but to witness.

The fox was already there.

Curled at the crest, its back to him, tail flicking in a lazy rhythm. It gazed up at the moon as if it had been waiting for him to arrive. The monk stepped closer. The roof groaned beneath his weight.

Then the fox shifted.

One paw nudged a loose shingle.

It skittered down the slope—clattering, sharp. A sound precise enough to cut straight through his thoughts.

The monk blinked.

And in that blink—he saw it.

The cabin wasn't tilting.

The moon hadn't moved.

Only he had.

He had spent days adjusting to a distortion that was never out there.

He sat beside the fox, still panting from the climb, heart unmoored.

The moonlight found the crown of his head and settled there, unmoved.

10

THE FOX THAT PLAYED DEAD

ONE PALE MORNING, THE MONK STEPPED OUT TO fetch water and found the fox lying at the edge of the clearing, its body curled in the grass, utterly still. One paw stretched forward. Eyes closed. Chest unmoving.

He stood for a long while, watching for breath.

Nothing.

He approached slowly, knees bending beside the small frame. He reached out—but before his fingers brushed fur, the fox sprang up, eyes gleaming, and dashed into the underbrush without a sound. A single white hair clung to the monk's sleeve.

The next day, it happened again.

A different spot this time—under the pine tree near the lantern, belly up, paws loose like marionette strings.

The monk's breath caught. He walked faster.

Again, the fox sprang to life and vanished.

On the third day, he didn't move at all. Just looked from the doorway, hands still damp from tea, and narrowed his eyes.

The fox opened one eye.

Then closed it again.

By the fourth morning, the monk found himself scanning the clearing before stepping outside. His chest felt tight, as if grief had arrived ahead of time, without invitation.

There it was, by the woodpile—limp, limbs folded neatly. So still it hurt to look at.

He approached quietly, crouched down, and whispered,

"You win."

Then turned and walked back inside.

He didn't see the fox lift its head, glance at the retreating figure, and let out a single bark—sharp and high, like a child stifling laughter.

On the fifth morning, the monk found no fox.

On the sixth, he did.

And this time, he didn't stop. He passed it without pause, without a glance. Just a soft bow as he stepped by.

The fox, belly to the sky, cracked open one eye. Then the other.

When no one looked, it smiled.

11

THE ROBE THAT WASN'T HIS

THE MONK AWOKE TO MIST AND THE SCENT OF wet leaves. He stood, stretched, and reached for his robe.

The wooden peg beside the door was empty.

He searched the cabin. Under the cushion. Beside the hearth. Behind the door.

Gone.

Wrapping a blanket around his shoulders, he stepped into the clearing. Dew clung to the grass like old silence. And then, at the edge of the woods, he saw it.

His robe—folded with care—rested on a low-hanging branch.

The fox was curled on top of it. Still. Eyes half-lidded. Watching nothing.

It didn't bolt. Didn't posture. It simply rose—graceful,

unconcerned—and walked past him without pause, as if he were no more threat than a breeze through reeds.

The monk felt something catch in his chest. Not fear. Something quieter. As if the fox saw through him, to something younger. Smaller.

He reached for the robe.

The fabric was soft, yes. Familiar. But when he lifted it, a weightless stillness settled over him.

Inside the collar, a faded emblem: a lotus inside a circle. Frayed. Pale.

He hadn't seen that mark in decades.

It was stitched into the robes worn by novices at the first monastery he resided at when he was barely more than a boy. His own robe had once carried that mark, long before silence became comfortable, before he had learned how to still his hands.

The smell was different—like dry sun and old sandalwood. The fabric felt impossibly light, as if woven from air, its edges shimmering faintly, like a memory refusing to settle.

He stared at it, and logic tried to form. Maybe he had packed it unknowingly. Maybe the fox had unearthed it from some hidden chest.

But those thoughts dissolved as he pressed the cloth to his chest.

His breath caught, a sob rising unbidden, as if the robe held the weight of a self he'd buried under years of discipline.

He took it inside and hung it gently. Watched the fabric sway slightly, though no wind touched it.

That evening, he dressed.

The robe settled over his shoulders with unnerving ease. He sat on the cushion, but it shifted under him—his posture unsteady, as if the robe pulled him back to a self he didn't know.

Memories surged.

Sixteen, bowing too quickly before a senior monk, only to feel a gentle hand correct his spine.

Pride, the first time he tied the knot without error.

Laughter in the corridor—his own—too loud, half-ashamed, fully alive.

He thought he had lost these things. He hadn't. They had only gone quiet.

Across the room, the fox batted a small rubber ball along the floor. It played with relentless ease, each tap of the ball a taunt to his unraveling mind.

He watched.

He realized he had changed. But something else had not.

Presence. The raw, unnameable is-ness beneath every

chant and gesture. The part of him that had always been watching, even when he didn't know what to look for.

The robe's lotus emblem caught the candle's glow, flaring like the fox's ball rolling into shadow.

He didn't know if the robe was his.

But it fit.

12

THE WRONG MONK

THE MONK WAS SITTING ON HIS CUSHION, EYES open but soft, breath following the rhythm of rustling leaves. It had been a quiet morning. The fox was nowhere in sight.

Then came the footsteps.

He turned his head slightly—just enough to see a man approaching through the trees. Mid-thirties. A woven hat. A basket slung over his shoulder. The man walked like someone with a mission, which in itself was suspicious.

When he saw the monk, the man stopped. Bowed low. Held the position for a beat too long.

"You must be the one who predicted the rains."

The monk blinked.

The man smiled reverently. "Three weeks ago. You sent

word through the river man, yes? Said the rains would come before the 12th full moon?"

The monk stood, slowly. "I sent no such word."

The man chuckled as if hearing a poem. "Ah, wisdom always plays shy. My village is speaking of you."

Before the monk could reply, a blur of red darted across the path behind the man. The fox. It paused just long enough to flash its teeth—something between a grin and a warning—then vanished again.

The man didn't seem to notice.

"We brought offerings," he continued, pulling out a scroll wrapped in red thread. "And a question. A boy in our village speaks riddles in his sleep. We were told you'd know what it means."

The monk looked around, expecting the trick to reveal itself—but the forest was silent.

Another figure arrived—an older woman this time, followed by a younger man with a flute. They, too, bowed.

By noon, six villagers had gathered. All waiting. All watching him with quiet awe.

The fox sat near the edge of the clearing now, tail wrapped neatly around its feet. Watching.

The monk cleared his throat. "There's been a mistake."

No one responded.

He stepped back into his cabin to buy time. The scroll lay on the table. Still sealed. He paced once. Twice.

Then, like smoke slipping under the door, the fox entered the room.

It didn't look at him.

Instead, it hopped onto the table, bit down on the scroll, and bolted.

The monk ran after it. The villagers followed him. Through the trees. Over the stream. Around the cabin once. Twice.

When they returned to the clearing, the scroll was gone. So was the fox.

Everyone stood there, breathless.

The older woman turned to the monk, eyes wide with something between fear and reverence. "He is wise," she whispered to the others. "He lets the answer run wild so we may chase it ourselves."

They bowed again. Then, one by one, left.

The monk sat down on his cushion. Heart still racing. Mind blank.

The fox returned just before sunset. It dropped a different scroll at his feet—blank parchment, curled slightly at the edges.

The monk opened it. Nothing.

He laughed.

Then sat straighter than he had all day.

13

THE CUP THAT FILLED ITSELF

NOTHING.

The monk had left his cup on the windowsill, as he always did, clean and empty, catching light.

That morning, when he returned from gathering water, the cup was full.

Not brimming—just the right amount, as if poured with care. The steam was still rising.

He stared at it for a long time. Touched it. Warm.

He tried to remember. Had he filled it and forgotten? No. He had gone straight to the stream, the path still damp with dew.

He brought the cup to his lips. Paused.

Then set it down.

The next day, it happened again.

The same cup. The same warmth. No sound of pouring. No kettle boiled. But the tea was there, just as before— still, golden, calm as a held breath.

He scanned the room. Nothing was out of place.

Except, of course, everything was.

By the third day, his hands trembled as he approached it.

The fox sat across the room that time, eyes half-lidded, body coiled but relaxed—like someone watching a story they already knew the end of.

The monk stepped back.

He whispered, "Is this your doing?"

The fox tilted its head.

He laughed once, dryly. "A fox that brews tea. Why not."

Then, more softly: "Or am I cursed?"

But the moment the word left his lips, he recoiled.

No. Not a curse. It didn't feel malevolent. It felt... precise. Measured. Like being watched by something that understood time differently.

Still, the wrongness curled around his thoughts like steam.

On the fourth day, he decided to catch it. He stayed in the room. Turned the cup upside down. Set it on the floor. Then sat with his back to the window.

Hours passed.

Nothing.

Eventually, he rose. Turned. Looked.

The cup was back on the sill. Upright. Full.

He hadn't heard a sound.

His breath caught. His stomach turned.

He lifted the cup.

It was warm. Fragrant.

He brought it to his lips, held it there for several long seconds.

Then drank.

It tasted like tea.

That was all.

Not bitter. Not sweet. Not strange.

Nothing shifted. No visions. No whispers. Just the faint heat moving down his throat, settling quietly into his belly.

He looked across the room.

The fox had curled into a ball, tail over its nose, already asleep.

The monk sat beside it, cup in hand, unsure whether he had just witnessed a miracle or forgotten how to remember something ordinary.

The tea remained warm for a long time.

14

THE MASTER WITH FOUR LEGS

He had been sending letters for months.

Whenever a villager passed through the clearing—delivering rice, offering herbs, asking nothing in return—the monk would press a folded slip of paper into their hand and say, "If your road takes you near the southern monastery, please leave this with the gatekeeper."

Each letter was written in the same spare, careful hand. Each addressed to the old master he had once studied under—whose voice still echoed in the back of his thoughts during long meditations.

The letters spoke not of achievement, but confusion.

He wrote of his retreat to the forest. Of silence gone strange. Of the fox—wild and half-seen, a riddle with paws. Of the things that disappeared, and reappeared different. Of the sense that something was watching him live a life he didn't understand.

And then, toward the end of one letter, he had added, almost impulsively:

"If you choose to visit, come on the night of the full moon. I'll leave the lamp lit."

The moon came and went. No reply.

He sent more letters. Never received one in return.

Then, one night, he prepared as if the master might come anyway.

He swept the floor three times. Lit incense. Set two cushions. Brewed tea from the older leaves—the kind reserved for guests who mattered.

The moon rose, full and bright, casting silver shadows against the walls. He waited.

And then—

There was a sound outside. Soft. Definite.

A figure approached through the clearing. Low to the ground. Fluid.

Not robes.

Fur.

The fox.

It stepped into the doorway without hesitation. Looked around the room slowly, as if evaluating the preparation. Its gaze rested on the two cushions. Then on the tea.

The monk felt disappointment rise through his chest like smoke that had lost its fire.

He had wanted it to be the master. He had imagined robes brushing the doorframe. A familiar voice clearing its throat. The weight of lineage entering the room like a second spine.

Instead, the fox sat across from him. On the empty cushion.

It did not blink.

The monk exhaled. Soft. Long. As if letting something go that had lingered too long in the lungs.

The fox closed its eyes.

The monk poured the tea. Only one cup. He didn't know why.

He drank it slowly.

Somewhere in that stillness—between breath, between sips—he felt something familiar settle around him. The weight of attention. The shape of presence. As if someone was watching him not to correct, but to witness.

Not a lesson. Not a koan.

Just the sense that nothing needed to be said.

He looked at the fox again.

The candlelight shifted slightly, and for the briefest

flicker—less than a blink—he could have sworn the face across from him was not entirely animal.

Then it was gone.

The fox stretched once. Rose. Walked slowly back into the dark.

The tea had grown cold.

But it didn't matter.

The cushion still held the shape of something that had once known how to bow.

15

THE SCAR THE FOX LEFT BEHIND

IT HAPPENED IN A BREATH. THE MONK TURNED the corner behind the cabin, arms full of kindling, not expecting movement. The fox was there—digging at the base of the path, ears back, tail rigid. It looked up. Flinched.

A blur of fur and light, then claws—not aimed, just flung —caught skin.

The kindling fell like startled birds, thudding against stone. The fox disappeared into the trees, a blur swallowed by leaves.

The monk stood still, his arm bleeding. The cut ran diagonal from forearm to elbow—a clean mark, vivid, stinging. As if the fox had opened a sentence and left it unfinished.

Inside, he washed it. Wrapped it. Tied the cloth too tight.

His fingers fumbled, tracing the wound again and again, as if he could undo the fox's stroke or force it to confess its intent.

The pain was slight, but the wound's sting gnawed, demanding a story he couldn't shape.

Was he careless? Too loud? Was it a message?

He turned the questions like a koan, each answer unmaking the one before it.

That night he dreamed of the fox's paw again—this time dipped in ink, scratching spirals on his chest.

Days passed. The wound closed. Left behind a thin red line like a river drawn from memory.

He thought that might be the end of it.

But at the stream one morning, as mist rose, he saw it: a fresh pawprint pressed into the soft bank, its edges sharp, recent, deliberate. Then the fox, across the water—still, watching.

The monk looked down at his scar. It pulsed faintly, a warm throb under the skin, as if the fox's claw had traced a map he couldn't yet read.

Their eyes met.

No apology. No blame. Only a shared gaze, sharp as the claw that cut him.

The fox blinked once. Turned. Vanished into the brush.

From the bend in the stream, a villager froze—basket in hand, her breath caught as she glimpsed the strange stillness across the water. A man and an animal. Silence louder than the river.

That night, the monk ran a finger along the scar, its red line catching the candle's flicker like a fox's tail in moonlight. It remained. But it no longer demanded answers.

16

———

THE PATH THAT SWALLOWED ITSELF

THE MONK HADN'T PLANNED TO FOLLOW IT.

He was stacking kindling near the edge of the clearing when the fox appeared again—just at the tree line, where shadow met sun. It looked at him, head tilted, and held the gaze longer than usual. Not with the flickering mischief it often carried, but with something stranger. Stillness.

Then it turned and walked into the woods with the certainty of one who knows they will be followed.

And he was.

The monk waited a moment, then took a breath and stepped after it. Not because he expected anything. Not really. Maybe he was curious? Yearning for an adventure? He wasn't quite sure himself.

He felt that the fox wasn't only tricking him—it was

leading him toward something he had once asked for and then forgotten.

The fox was already gone by the time he reached the trees. But there, pressed into the soft dirt, was a trail of pawprints. Small. Perfect. Leading forward.

He followed.

The forest thickened around him, not ominous, but watchful. Light dappled the undergrowth in uneasy patterns. The pawprints curled ahead of him in a loose spiral, never rushing, never doubling back.

A strange silence settled. No birdsong. Just wind and breath and the sound of his own feet trying not to make noise.

At one point, he stepped on something soft. He looked down.

A sock. Worn thin at the heel. Child-sized.

He left it where it lay.

Further in, he passed a squirrel perched on a branch, holding a pinecone in both paws, completely still. Its eyes followed him, unblinking, as though judging the worth of his journey.

He bowed to it. The squirrel did not respond.

The trail bent again, circling what looked like the same tree he had passed minutes ago—though now it was covered in moss he didn't remember. Or maybe the moss had always been there, and he had forgotten how to see it.

He kept walking.

Then, at the base of a flat stone, he saw it.

An apple. Red. Bitten once. No teeth marks. Just the crescent of the bite, clean and bright.

He crouched beside it. Looked up.

The clearing.

His cabin.

The path had returned him.

The prints led no further.

He stood in silence, unsure whether he had followed something real, or merely moved in circles.

Then a laugh—not loud, not close—rippled through the trees. It bounced between trunks, playful, teasing, impossible to place. He turned, but the forest was already quiet again.

He looked down at the apple.

Behind him, footsteps.

He turned and saw a woman standing at the edge of the clearing, a woven basket in her arms, filled with herbs and leaves he didn't recognize. Her eyes widened when she saw him.

"Oh," she said softly. "So you are real."

He said nothing.

"I've heard of you," she continued. "The one who lives at the edge of the loop. They say if you walk the wrong way in these woods, you find yourself back here. But I thought it was just a story."

The monk glanced at the trail behind him, now disappearing in the rising breeze.

"I thought it was a teaching," she added, adjusting her basket. "But maybe it's just the way the world is."

She bowed and walked past him, quiet as a falling leaf.

The monk remained still. Then sat beside the apple. He picked it up. Held it in his palm. Then set it back down where he found it.

He didn't feel tricked.

Not entirely.

He wasn't sure what he felt.

But his legs stayed ready. The path had swallowed itself, yes—but something inside him had been stirred.

And somewhere, not far, the fox was already watching again.

17

THE FOX THAT ASKED FOR TEA

ONE AFTERNOON, THE MONK PLACED TWO CUPS on the porch.

He didn't know why. Perhaps a gesture to the forest. Perhaps habit. The cup sat opposite his own, steam rising quietly, curling into the air like a question left unanswered.

The fox approached without hurry. Paused at the step. Looked at the cup. Then at the monk. Then back to the cup.

It sat.

The monk poured.

The fox dipped its paw in the tea, then licked it. Its face twisted as if it had bitten into something far too honest.

It walked off.

The next day, the monk added a sprig of mint. The fox sniffed it, sneezed, and left without even a glance.

Ginger. Mushrooms. A sliver of honey bark. Each day a new offering. Each day the fox came, tasted, and left unsatisfied. Once it yawned. Once it curled up next to the cup and napped, untouched.

The monk began to enjoy the ritual. Not the success. Not the tea. The attempt.

Then, one grey morning, tired and unsure, he offered only warm water.

The fox drank the entire thing. Sat a while. Longer than usual. It didn't look at him. Didn't look away.

When it finally left, it knocked over the monk's cup with its tail.

The monk didn't mind. He picked up the empty cup and drank what wasn't there.

Reflection Questions

FOR BEGINNERS

Have you ever tried to fix something—not because it was broken, but because its uncertainty made you uncomfortable?

What do you carry that no one else can see, but you still feel pulsing beneath the surface?

When was the last time something ordinary felt sacred—and did you notice, or only understand it later?

What are you really chasing when you seek answers? And what might be waiting if you stopped?

PART III
The Teacher and The Trickster

THE SECRET TO ZEN IS JUST TWO WORDS: NOT ALWAYS SO.

Shunryu Suzuki

18

—

THE DAY THE FOX WASN'T REAL

IT WAS A STRANGE DAY.

The monk had been watching the fox walk across the clearing, backlit by early sun, when he noticed something was missing.

There was no shadow. No shape stretching behind it. No outline responding to light. Just fur and movement and the sound of leaves giving way beneath four silent paws.

He blinked. It was still there—fox, yes. But no shadow. None at all.

The fox sat and licked its shoulder, as if unaware of its own impossibility.

That evening, the monk tried not to think about it. He swept the floor. Lit the lamp. Cooked a bit of rice. He even meditated longer than usual, hoping the breath would clear the confusion.

Then came the voice.

It wasn't loud. Just close.

He opened his eyes. Looked around.

Nothing.

But as he turned to extinguish the lamp, he heard it again —low, playful, entirely unfamiliar.

"Why do you breathe like you own the air?"

He spun. No one there.

He slept lightly that night, one ear tilted toward silence. Just before dawn, he dreamt of the fox sitting in his room, curled atop the cushion, asking questions in a tongue he didn't know but somehow understood.

"Why do you look for footprints when you could follow the wind?"

The monk answered in the dream. Or maybe just nodded.

He woke confused. And sweating.

He stepped outside for air.

Above the cabin, dew still clung to the wooden roof. The light was just enough to see it: a pawprint, pressed into the center of the slanted boards—on the ceiling.

No mud. No dirt. Just the shape. Clear and sharp, like something had walked upside down while he slept.

He leaned back, staring at it until his neck ached.

Later that day, he saw the fox again.

It was sitting on a tree branch. And beside it—calm, unbothered—an owl.

The two were facing each other.

As if in conversation.

The owl hooted once. The fox responded with a twitch of its tail and something that might've been a nod. Then both turned and looked down at him.

The monk waved.

The owl blinked. The fox didn't.

That night, he dreamt again.

"Why do you keep trying to wake up," the fox said, "when it's the dream that's been watching you?"

He woke before he could answer.

The pawprint was gone.

The shadow had returned.

The owl was nowhere to be seen.

19

———

THE LANGUAGE THAT WASN'T SHARED

THE MONK HAD DECIDED IT WAS TIME TO understand the fox.

Truly understand. Not just observe its movements or infer its moods. He wanted to speak to it. Connect. Bridge the gap.

So he began with words.

"Hello," he said, bowing.

The fox scratched its ear.

"Do you understand?"

The fox blinked slowly, then rolled onto its back.

Undeterred, the monk tried sound. One evening, he crouched just outside the cabin and barked.

Loudly.

Once. Twice.

Then a third time, with more depth.

The forest went quiet.

The fox, sitting nearby, let out a soft huff. Then another.

Then something between a sneeze and a wheeze—and then the unmistakable sound of laughing. Shoulders bouncing. Mouth open. Tongue lolling.

The monk turned red.

The next day, he tried movement. He crept on all fours, tailing the fox. When the fox stopped, he stopped. When the fox squatted, he squatted.

When the fox curled up and licked its side, the monk paused. Considered.

Then politely turned away.

Still, the fox did not leave. Which, to the monk, meant he was getting somewhere.

One morning, exhausted but determined, he knelt in front of the fox and asked, "What do I have to do to understand you?"

The fox stared at him. Then disappeared into the underbrush.

The monk sighed. He remained kneeling, eyes closed, trying not to hope.

Something thumped beside him.

He opened his eyes.

A dead mouse.

Not torn, not mangled. Just... delivered. Neatly.

The monk stared at it. Then at the fox, who now sat with its tail swaying casually, as if offering the most reasonable answer in the world.

"You want me to eat this?" the monk asked.

The fox yawned. Loudly.

The monk didn't eat the mouse. But he carried it to the edge of the woods and buried it with a small chant, unsure who the ceremony was for.

That night, he didn't bark. He didn't copy. He didn't ask.

He sat.

The fox came close, circled him once, then curled up beside his cushion. Their backs just barely touching.

And in that closeness, a strange understanding bloomed.

No word had been spoken.

No meaning clarified.

But something had arrived between them—soft, warm, and complete.

20

———

THE SHARED MEAL

It was a homesick kind of evening.

The monk didn't miss people. Not exactly. But something quieter. The smell of warm rice. The hush of steam rising from bowls. The clink of chopsticks laid gently on wood. The rhythm of shared meals, even in silence.

So, he cooked.

Not to nourish. Not to meditate. Just to remember.

A stew—thin but fragrant, laced with ginger and dried herbs, the way he'd had it during long winter nights at the monastery. He portioned two bowls. Out of habit, or hope, he didn't know.

He set them on the low table, lit a candle, and sat cross-legged in the glow.

The clearing rustled.

A flash of red.

The fox stepped into the light. Not slowly. Not cautiously. Just... directly. As if this had been planned.

It padded over to the second bowl and, without hesitation, **devoured the contents**—slurping, chewing, licking the rim clean.

The monk blinked.

He let out a small laugh. Not because it was funny. Because it was absurd. And somehow perfect.

He turned back to his own bowl.

Empty.

Steam still hung in the air above it. But the food was gone.

The fox was gone too.

The candle flickered.

He sat there a long while, full of nothing he could name.

21

THE RIVER THAT TURNED AROUND

THE MONK WOKE TO A STRANGE QUIET. NOT silence exactly—just something missing.

He stepped outside. The ground was damp. A thick line of mist drifted along the tree trunks, curling low across the forest floor.

He walked toward the stream. Leaves crackled underfoot. Birds rustled in the canopy above, but none called out.

At the river's edge, he crouched.

The water was moving upstream.

The current bent against its usual path. A branch floated past him, heading the wrong way. Smooth, steady, certain.

He scanned the banks for a blockage—nothing. Stones were still. The riverbed unchanged.

He looked up.

Across the stream, a fox sat between two moss-covered roots. Watching. Tail draped to one side, ears flicking. Its eyes followed the water, then turned toward him.

A sound broke behind him.

The wind rustled in reverse. Leaves that had fallen now tumbled up the hill.

Smoke twisted downward from the cabin chimney, coiling into the ground.

A bird flapped past him—its wings pushing back instead of forward. It landed on a branch, paused, then launched straight up, vanishing through the trees.

He gripped a nearby rock. Cold, solid. His breath grew shallow.

The river slowed.

Then it shifted. A pause in the current. The water hung for a moment—neither backward nor forward—then resumed its usual course, slipping downstream as if nothing had changed.

The fox stood. It gave a sharp yip—high, quick—almost like a bark.

Then it turned and disappeared into the underbrush.

The monk stayed a little longer, staring at the water.

On the way back, he noticed his footprints in the mud.

They were facing toward the stream, but the heel marks came first.

When he stepped inside the cabin, his robe was already folded.

Backwards.

22

———

THE TRAP THAT WAS ALREADY EMPTY

THE FOX HAD STOLEN NOTHING LATELY.

No apples from the basket. No bite marks on the monk's lunch. No pawprints across the cushion or mud on the windowsill.

And that, the monk decided, was suspicious.

So, one morning, he set a simple trap—just a wooden crate tilted on a stick, a slice of melon beneath it, and a string coiled loosely around his wrist as he meditated nearby.

Not to harm the fox. Just to catch it for a moment. To look it in the eyes and ask what all this meant.

Hours passed. He sat. The sun arced slowly overhead.

No rustle. No snap.

Then, just as dusk began to settle, he felt the faintest tug on the string.

His hand moved quickly.

The crate fell.

He rose, heartbeat tapping against his ribs.

When he approached the trap, it looked perfect—centered, collapsed over the bait.

But inside: nothing.

The melon slice was gone. The stick still in place. The string unmoved.

He lifted the crate.

No pawprints. No trail. No fox.

Just beneath the crate, resting on the dirt, was a scrap of bark.

Scratched into its surface, in crude, uneven strokes, was a short poem:

No catch.

No proof.

The shadow eats its tail—

You're holding the wrong string.

The monk ran a thumb over the marks. Some of the letters were backwards. Some were barely legible.

He didn't know if the fox wrote it. Or if it was meant for him.

But he kept it.

That evening, he sat by the window, turning the bark over in his hand as the fire cracked.

Outside, the fox passed by. It didn't stop, didn't look in.

It only flicked its tail once, slow and deliberate, before vanishing again.

23

———

THE STONE THAT WOULDN'T LEAVE

IT WASN'T A SPECIAL STONE.

Just a lump of granite, round on one side, flat on the other, and shaped vaguely like a fist. The monk noticed it one morning in the middle of the path—right where he walked barefoot from the cabin to the stream.

He moved it to the side.

The next day, it was back.

He frowned, picked it up, and tossed it deeper into the woods. Not hard, but far enough it wouldn't be found again by accident.

The next morning, it sat exactly where it had been. Same side up. Same spot.

The monk looked around. The forest said nothing. The fox was nowhere in sight.

This time he buried it. Dug a hole with a stick, pressed it deep, covered it with packed earth, leaves, and a flat rock.

The next morning, it was back.

Now he watched. Spent the evening sitting by the door, eyes on the path. Hours passed. Stars gathered and dissolved. The wind shifted once or twice.

Nothing moved.

And still, in the morning, the stone was there.

He tried offerings—placing a bowl of rice next to it. The rice was gone by sunrise. The stone remained.

He tried warning signs—marking the path with twigs in strange patterns, circling the stone with ash. That night, it rained.

The next morning, the stone sat clean and dry, untouched by the storm.

He tried forgetting. Stepped over it. Ignored it. Let it sit there for days.

But the thing about ignoring something is that it knows. It waits.

Eventually, he gave up.

One morning, without ceremony, he sat down beside it. Not in defeat, but in silence. He touched the stone. It was smooth, cool. Slightly damp from the mist.

He didn't speak. Didn't question.

From the trees, the fox padded into view. It approached, sniffed the stone, and—without hesitation—lay down beside it, curling its tail around its body.

The monk watched for a while, then lay down too.

The sun passed overhead. The birds chattered. A light breeze stirred the leaves.

When he rose, the stone was gone.

He never looked for it again.

24

———

THE FIRE THAT DANCED BACK

THE MONK BUILT THE FIRE DIFFERENTLY THAT evening.

He didn't need the warmth. The night was gentle. But something inside him pressed against stillness—an itch, not of restlessness, but return. He moved through the clearing with a slow urgency, gathering wood from the cedar's roots, choosing pieces that felt right in the hand.

His chest tightened as he knelt to build it. A strange resistance bloomed inside him—fear, maybe, of being seen, even in the dark. His hands shook slightly as he placed the first log.

A faint pawprint circled the fire's edge, pressed deep into the earth. As if the fox had already been there. As if it had traced the spiral first.

He lit the match.

The flames caught slowly, like breath relearning how to begin. They twisted upward, forming different shapes and symbols before dissolving into sparks that hovered in the air too long to be natural.

He stepped back.

Then forward.

He began to move—not as a dancer, not with grace. Just motion, pulled from the joints. A tilt of the shoulder. A lean. His feet shifted without plan, drawing uneven circles around the fire. The flames flickered toward him. The air pulled away.

A ritual had begun.

A ritual with no meaning and music.

Then a shadow moved with him. Or ahead of him.

The fox.

It circled opposite him, swift and low, its body carving tighter spirals. Its speed pulled something loose from the monk's rhythm—he stumbled, almost fell, his foot catching on the edge of his own momentum.

The fox didn't slow.

His breath hitched. His limbs flared out to catch himself. He nearly stopped—but didn't.

Instead, he leaned into the wobble. Let it carry him forward. Something broke inside his pacing—a rhythm that wasn't his own, but that welcomed him like an old drumbeat rediscovered.

As he regained his balance, the fox slowed too. Their movements—no longer mirrored, but resonant—wove together like smoke finding its way through trees.

He stopped.

The fox stopped.

He bowed his head—as if not knowing how else to end.

The fox sat, its gaze steady, the flames painting gold across its fur.

He lowered himself to the ground.

The fire crackled once—louder than expected—then settled.

The monk looked down. The pawprint beside him had blurred.

He felt something shift in his spine.

That night, the fire burned lower. The clearing breathed slower. The stars blinked like they were trying to remember a dream.

NO

25

—

THE LOG THAT SAID NO

THE MONK HAD BEEN ASKING TOO MANY questions.

Not aloud, perhaps, but inside—where the mind runs even when the mouth stays shut.

Questions that churned:

Was the fox his teacher?

Was this all illusion?

Was he closer now, or further away?

One morning, he stood at the edge of the clearing, hands folded behind his back, and asked the fox plainly:

"Are you here to teach me?"

The fox looked up from licking its paw.

Then turned away.

That night, the monk dreamed he was chasing an answer through fog. Each time he reached for it, it dissolved like steam. When he woke, his knees ached, and he couldn't remember why.

He stepped outside to clear his head.

And there it was.

A log.

Too thick to have rolled there by accident. Set directly in front of the cabin door. Square and deliberate, like a punctuation mark. He had to step over it to pass.

He checked the woodshed. No logs missing. He hadn't cut this one.

He went closer to inspect.

Carved into the bark—rough, unmistakable—was a single word:

No.

He stared at it for a long time.

He couldn't remember what question it had answered.

Or how long he'd been staring.

But each time he passed it, he asked something. Quietly.

"Is this all a game?"

"Am I still dreaming?"

"Have I misunderstood everything?"

Each day, the log remained still.

And the word, carved into its dry bark, unchanged.

The fox watched from a distance, tail twitching slightly —amused, maybe. Or just present.

The next day, after an evening walk, the monk stopped at the log before entering the cabin.

He bowed.

Then stepped over it, and went inside.

Reflection Questions

What has disappeared from your life but still seems to leave a presence behind?

What in your life have you passed by many times without truly seeing?

What if what you long for is already here, just out of reach?

What questions are you carrying that cannot be answered with words?

PART IV
The Fading Fox

THE QUIETER YOU BECOME, THE MORE YOU CAN HEAR.

Zen Proverb

26

———

THE FOX THAT WORE A HAT

He hadn't worn the hat in years.

It hung behind the door, sun-bleached and frayed, but still intact. Woven straw, rim wide enough to shade the eyes.

A monk's hat, yes, but not just any. It had been gifted to him long ago by a friend he no longer wrote to—one of those people you carry in silence, even after the voices fade.

It was a gift.

She had given it to him at the foot of a dry mountain. No parting words. Only a nod and the pressing of palm to palm. He had worn it every day until one afternoon, deep in the forest, he simply stopped.

Hung it up and closed the door.

Now, this morning, that door creaked open all on its own.

And sitting just beyond the step—legs neatly folded beneath him, tail curled like a question mark, hat perfectly balanced atop his head—was the fox.

The monk stared.

The fox didn't blink.

The straw hat looked too large for its narrow skull, but somehow it stayed in place, slanted low like it had something to hide.

The fox tilted its head just slightly, the brim tipping with it, and then, slowly, the fox turned and trotted off into the woods—hat bobbing atop its head like it had always belonged there.

The monk followed.

Not quickly. Not with anger. But with something else rising in his chest. Something like grief, warmed at the edges by laughter.

The forest was brighter than usual, every leaf catching too much light.

Each time he glimpsed the fox, it was just far enough ahead to vanish again.

As he walked, he found a scrap of cloth snagged on a branch.

It wasn't the fox's. It was part of his old traveling robe. He hadn't seen it in decades.

Another turn revealed a set of parallel stones—like old temple steps.

His old friend's name flashed across his mind.

He could see her then, kneeling by a stream, dipping the hat into the water to cool it before pressing it to his neck. He remembered her laughter—gentle, always a little bit ahead of him.

The fox reappeared, watching him from a low ridge. The monk climbed toward it.

And just before the summit, the fox dropped the hat.

It tumbled once. Landed upright on the moss.

The monk reached it, panting, the memory of years thick in his chest. He picked it up. The inside was dry, warm. He held it close. The scent was no longer dust or straw.

It was her.

The fox was gone.

He sat down on the ridge. Below, the trees swayed without wind. The hat rested in his lap. His hands trembled.

It wasn't a memory. It wasn't grief.

It was presence, woven into straw and silence.

The monk placed the hat on his head.

It didn't quite fit.

But it felt right.

27

THE TRAIL OF TEETH

It started off as a normal morning.

The monk had been out early, gathering mushrooms after a night of mist. The ground was soft, clinging to his sandals. As he stooped beneath a cedar's arching roots, he saw it—a tooth.

Small, curved. Still white, but aged at the root.

He pocketed it without thought.

But then he found another, lodged in a tree stump like a splinter of the moon.

And another, at the base of a stone, just beside a fox's pawprint.

He crouched lower, tracing the line they formed. A path.

Teeth led him between trees, across the shallow creek, and into a part of the forest where bark flaked like old paint and the air seemed to hum.

Each tooth was slightly different—some jagged, some polished smooth. Some still red at the base, as if freshly shed.

The trail felt deliberate.

He thought about predators. A wolf, perhaps. Or something worse, something older. His heartbeat didn't quicken, but the skin on his arms felt pulled tight.

Halfway through the trail, he stopped. There, pressed into the damp earth, was a massive molar—larger than any animal of the woods should bear.

A breeze passed then, cold and brief. The forest exhaled.

The monk stood in silence, unsure whether to go forward. That's when he heard it—high and thin, nearly a whistle.

Laughter.

He turned sharply.

A few feet behind him sat the fox, watching.

It yawned. Then licked its teeth.

The monk opened his mouth to speak—then closed it again.

The fox turned. Vanished into the trees.

He looked down.

The trail was gone.

The teeth—gone.

Even the giant sunk into the soil, swallowed like it had never existed.

He checked his robe pocket.

Empty.

All that remained was the faint memory of crunching beneath his feet.

That night, he dreamed of biting into an apple and finding a tooth inside.

The next morning, his mouth tasted of iron.

But his own teeth were all still there.

28

THE VILLAGER WITH THE FOX TATTOO

She arrived at dusk with a bundle of firewood, her stride slow and certain, like she'd crossed seasons to reach him.

The monk was sweeping the porch. He'd seen her before from afar—always passing the edge of the forest, always alone. But today, she came straight to him, set the firewood down, and stretched her arms with a sigh that carried seasons.

"Thought your fire might be tired," she said.

He offered tea. She accepted without hesitation.

They sat on the porch. The fox lay a few feet away, tail coiled neatly around its paws, pretending not to listen.

That's when he saw it—her sleeve slipped up as she reached for the cup. A tattoo on her forearm. Faded but unmistakable: a fox, inked in sweeping black lines, its tail curling around a full moon.

He tried not to stare, but failed.

"You've met him, then," she said, not looking up.

"The fox?" the monk asked.

"No," she replied. "The question."

He blinked. "What does it mean?"

She ran a finger along the rim of her cup. "I got it after my first real silence. Not the kind where you stop talking. The kind where everything else stops talking back."

The monk waited, unsure if more would come.

She continued. "The fox was never there to be tamed. It's the wind that circles before you notice the weather's changed. It's the missing sock, the extra heartbeat. It's the part of you that doesn't answer to you."

"I don't understand," the monk admitted.

She smiled. "That's because you're still asking."

The monk looked down at his hands. "But if I stop—"

"Then you'll hear him clearer." She stood, brushing dust from her trousers. "Or not. He doesn't always like being heard."

The fox lifted its head now. Watched her.

As she turned to leave, she called back, "You'll know it's time to stop chasing him when he starts chasing you."

And then she vanished into the trees, same as she came— no rustle, no trail.

The monk sat with his tea until it cooled.

Later, when he looked again, the fox was gone.

But etched faintly into the porch wood, as if someone had dragged a thumb through ash, was a small curling shape.

A tail.

Or a question mark.

He didn't touch it. He just sat a little longer, waiting to see what else might show up.

29

THE LOG THAT SPLIT ITSELF

THE MONK HAD AWAKENED EARLY TO SPLIT firewood.

The axe was old, its wooden handle worn smooth from years of repetition. He liked the sound it made—clean, direct, honest. The log pile behind the cabin had grown unruly again, and this too, he thought, was practice.

He raised the axe. Breathed in. Breathed out.

Then swung.

The axe bounced off the first log with a dull thunk. He examined the edge. Sharp enough. Just...stubborn wood.

He tried again.

Thunk.

By the third swing, he was sweating. By the fifth, muttering. By the seventh, contemplating impermanence and the fleeting nature of patience.

A rustle behind him.

The fox. Sitting by the edge of the forest. Watching. Tail curled neatly. Head tilted.

The monk wiped his brow. "You're welcome to help."

The fox blinked slowly.

He expected the fox to sit and watch again. Instead, it nosed at the axe, sniffed it, then gnawed once at the wooden handle with its sharp teeth—just a test bite. Then it trotted away into the trees.

The monk shook his head and turned back to the log. "Before enlightenment, chop wood," he muttered. "After enlightenment—"

CRACK.

The log split.

But not from the axe. He hadn't touched it.

He stared. The two halves lay perfectly even, like they'd been waiting all along to separate.

Behind him, the fox was gone.

He checked the woodshed. Empty. No sign of the fox. No footprints. Nothing disturbed.

Except the next log in the pile—cracked down the middle, split as cleanly as the first.

He didn't swing again.

Just sat beside the stack of logs.

Let the axe rest beside him.

And laughed.

30

———

THE DAY OF LAUGHTER

THAT MORNING, THE MONK WAS UNUSUALLY serious.

He swept the porch with the intensity of a general preparing for war. He straightened the cushion five times, each time with less satisfaction. He adjusted his robe until the folds lined up exactly as they did in the scrolls.

He sat. He inhaled. He prepared to enter vast silence.

Around 5 minutes into his meditation, he sneezed.

The sneeze echoed like thunder across the clearing. A bird flew off in alarm. The fox, curled under the porch, made a sound suspiciously close to a snort.

The monk rubbed his nose. Ignored it.

He returned to his breath. Counted three full inhalations. Four.

Then a sound: **Pffft.**

The fox stared at him.

The monk stared back.

The fox's tail twitched once. Then again. Then it rolled onto its side, legs flopping in the air like a poorly carved statue.

The monk tried to suppress a smile.

Failed.

He looked away, but everything was wrong. The pine tree beside the cabin had a curve he'd never noticed—like it was trying to dance.

The clouds were shaped like dumplings.

And a mushroom, growing near the porch, *bounced*. Not swayed. Bounced. As if enjoying its own joke.

The monk blinked. The mushroom winked.

He got up to inspect it. Stepped on a twig. It made the exact sound of a hiccup. He hiccuped in response. That made him laugh.

The laugh startled a squirrel, who dropped a pinecone, which hit the fox, who yelped and scampered in a wide circle before leaping onto the porch and depositing a sandal on the monk's head.

Now the monk was wearing a sandal crown, giggling like a child lost in the market.

He fell backward, gasping, tears running down his cheeks. Laughed at his own legs, at the clouds, at the bouncing mushroom, at the fox now bowing with exaggerated grace like an actor at the end of a play.

Then, between hiccups and snorts, the monk felt something else slip free. A small weight he hadn't known he was holding. A tightness around his breath. A seriousness that once felt like discipline, now dissolving into nonsense.

He laughed louder. Louder still.

And then—

Pfffffrrrrrrpp.

The fox farted.

It was long. Triumphant. Possibly musical.

The monk howled with laughter. He couldn't stop. He rolled on the ground, clutching his belly, choking on joy. The fox applauded with its paws.

Eventually, the laughter softened into silence.

The kind of silence that doesn't try to be quiet.

The kind that simply is.

31

———

WHERE THE FOX TOUCHED HIM

THE MONK COULDN'T NAME THE SENSATION HE had been feeling all day.

No pain, no dream. Just a warmth on his right shoulder, as if something had rested there for hours.

He sat up slowly. The cabin was quiet. The sun had not yet reached the floorboards. And yet he felt... watched.

He turned.

Nothing.

Just the cushion. The kettle. The low window.

But the sensation pulsed—gentle, persistent—on the back of his shoulder.

He stood and removed his robe.

Nothing. No wound. No bruise. Not even the faintest change in the skin. He pressed a hand to the spot. Still warm. As if the air itself had left a fingerprint.

He stepped outside.

The fox sat at the edge of the clearing, watching. Its tail was wrapped neatly around its legs. Its ears were still, eyes unreadable. It looked at the monk the way wind looks at trees: not waiting for a reply, only listening.

The monk raised his hand. The fox rose.

It padded forward, then circled him once, close enough to touch but never brushing. It stopped beside the same shoulder, tilted its head—then turned and walked into the trees.

The monk followed.

He moved like someone walking through a memory.

The path narrowed. The trees leaned closer. Somewhere above, a crow gave a single caw, sharp and irrelevant. The monk ducked under a low branch and found himself at the stream. Mist clung to its edges, and the stones beneath the surface looked like teeth.

The fox was gone.

He sat on a boulder and let his feet touch the water. Cool. Clear. Running the right direction, at least.

The warmth in his shoulder had faded.

But something else stirred. Not quite sadness. Not quite wonder.

He looked over his shoulder again.

Still nothing.

Back at the cabin, the sensation returned. A presence, just behind him. As if someone had followed but stopped just short of the porch.

He turned.

This time, he saw movement.

Not the fox.

Grass bending, gently, in a slow spiral. As if something unseen had walked in a circle. Right around the spot where he had stood.

He stepped out and walked to it. Nothing there. But his shoulder tingled again.

He went back inside and opened the small wooden box beneath his cushion—the one where he sometimes kept letters, folded thoughts, or bits of forest that refused to leave him.

He found a small mirror.

He held it up to the spot on his shoulder.

Still nothing.

But he smiled.

He didn't know why.

He only knew that he had stopped asking.

That night, the fox did not come.

But the next morning, a single tuft of red fur sat on the porch, beside a cluster of mushrooms that hadn't been there the day before. No pawprints. No breeze. Just the fur and the fungi, like an offering.

He bent to pick up the fur, but stopped.

Instead, he sat beside it.

The warmth on his shoulder returned, faint now. Faint, but constant.

The fox never touched him.

And yet something had.

32

———

THE TREE THAT LAUGHED FIRST

A sound.

Like a soft crack of bark splitting as the sun warmed the cedar at the far edge of the clearing. The monk paused mid-sip of his tea. He'd passed that tree a hundred times, maybe more, never once thinking it had anything to say.

But today, the sound echoed strangely.

Not like splitting wood. Not like a bird call.

More like a laugh. The kind the fox would give when it knocked over his water pot or dropped pinecones onto his head from the roof. That hiccuped rhythm. Dry. Precise. Mischievous.

He turned to look.

The tree stood in place. Crooked as always. Shadows clung to its trunk. Nothing unusual.

He smiled a little. Shook his head.

The next morning, it happened again. This time while he was sweeping the porch.

Crack.

Just once. Just enough.

He stopped. Waited. Nothing.

He walked over to touch the bark.

But in the stillness, he felt watched. Or maybe remembered. He couldn't decide which.

On the third day, the forest joined in.

One crack came from the cedar. Another from a pine across the stream. Then a pop from a branch overhead. Each time, the sound rippled through the clearing like stifled laughter.

He found himself laughing too. Not out loud. Not yet. But a bubbling in his chest rose whenever he heard it.

He never saw the fox during these moments. But the feeling of being watched grew stronger.

One night, a villager passing through the woods paused to greet him. They spoke briefly. As she turned to go, she hesitated. Looked over his shoulder.

"Something just moved in that tree," she said. "I thought it looked like a red tail."

He didn't turn to look.

Instead, he walked into the clearing, back to the cedar, and sat.

He didn't ask for anything. Not this time.

He simply sat.

The wind stirred.

Then the bark cracked again. Louder. This time unmistakable.

A warm, clicking giggle.

The sound moved through the trunk, into the ground beneath him, then up into his chest. And suddenly, it didn't matter whether it was the fox, or the tree, or something else altogether.

He let out a breath.

One he hadn't noticed he'd been holding.

The light began to shift. Evening crept in through the leaves. But he stayed. The roots beneath him felt soft, like folded cloth.

He stayed until the sky turned dark, and when the sound of laughter grew quiet.

When he stood, the moss beneath his feet felt lighter.

He looked once more at the cedar. A patch of bark had peeled away during the day. It revealed a shape.

Not quite a pawprint. But close.

He smiled.

33

———

THE FOX WHO TAUGHT ZEN

HE HAD NOT SEEN THE FOX IN WEEKS.

No flick of tail in the grass. No pawprints on the porch. No bite marks on apples or laughter in the dark.

The monk went about his days as usual—chopping wood, warming stew, sitting in the stillness—but something in the quiet had shifted. The silence no longer asked for listening. It simply was.

One afternoon, walking down the hill toward the riverbed for fresh water, the monk saw someone in the field: a villager he'd passed once or twice before, gathering mushrooms with a practiced hand and a keen eye.

She noticed him and straightened, brushing soil from her fingers. "Strange to see a monk this far out," she said, with no judgment. "You live nearby?"

"I do," he said. "A cabin, just over the ridge."

"Ah," she nodded, then added with a curious smile, "Is it true, what they say about that forest?"

He tilted his head. "What do they say?"

"That there's a fox who lives there. A clever one. Been there for generations. Plays tricks on monks, or so the old stories go."

The monk blinked. "What kind of tricks?"

She shrugged. "Depends on the monk. Some were annoyed. Others got angry. A few left crying."

The monk paused. "I know that fox."

She looked at him. "Do you?"

"Yes. I think so."

She smiled wider, as if something had just been confirmed. "Then I guess you're one of his students."

The monk hesitated. "I don't know what he's teaching me anymore. I haven't seen him in weeks."

The villager wiped her hands on her apron, then looked up at the clouds. "Must be a new lesson then," she said simply. And with that, she picked up her basket and walked away.

He stood there a long time after she left. Watching the wind move through the tall grass. Listening to the ordinary sounds of the forest.

He didn't understand. But he didn't resist the not-knowing either.

That night, sitting by the fire, the monk remembered all the places the fox had shown up. All the moments of laughter, confusion, frustration. All the marks the fox had left—some visible, some not.

He didn't dream that night.

The next morning, he packed his things and left.

The stillness no longer needed to be filled. The questions could stay with no answer.

As he stepped off the porch, a breeze lifted through the trees. In it, maybe—just maybe—he heard a laugh.

But he didn't look back.

FOR BEGINNERS

Can you sit with the arrival of mystery without rushing to name it?

Can you bow to something you do not understand?

What does it feel like to honor something without needing to replace it?

What if nothing needs to arrive for the moment to be complete?

Thank you for taking the time to read *The Fox Who Fooled The Monk*. My hope is that these stories have brought you moments of stillness, clarity, or even a small shift in perspective.

This book is part of a larger journey—to share the wisdom of Zen in a simple, accessible way so that more people can experience its teachings and find peace in their lives. In a world that often feels chaotic, even a single story can be a stepping stone to stillness.

If you found value in this book, I'd really appreciate it if you could leave an honest review. Your feedback helps others discover these teachings.

Scan the QR Code or click here to share your thoughts.

Thank you for being part of this journey.

— Kai

References

Kapleau, Philip. *The Three Pillars of Zen: Teaching, Practice, and Enlightenment.* New York: Anchor Books, 1989.

Reps, Paul, and Nyogen Senzaki. *Zen Flesh, Zen Bones: A Collection of Zen and Pre-Zen Writings.* Boston: Tuttle Publishing, 1998.

Shunryu, Suzuki. *Zen Mind, Beginner's Mind.* New York: Shambhala Publications, 2006.

Watts, Alan. *The Way of Zen.* New York: Vintage Books, 1957.

Yamada, Koun. *Zen: The Authentic Gate.* Somerville, MA: Wisdom Publications, 2015.

Mark Morse, trans. *The Gateless Gate: The Classic Book of Zen Koans.* Berkeley: Counterpoint, 2019.

Zen Training: Methods and Philosophy. By Katsuki Sekida. Boston: Shambhala Publications, 2005.

www.ingramcontent.com/pod-product-compliance
Lightning Source LLC
Chambersburg PA
CBHW021713190726
48289CB00008B/2502